For all who chase their dreams.
—ISN

Library of Congress Cataloging-in-Publication Data available.

ISBN 978-1-4521-5608-8

Manufactured in China.

Design by Kristine Brogno.
Typeset in Italia Book.
The illustrations in this book were rendered in
ink and color pencil and composited digitally.

10 9 8 7 6 5 4 3 2 1

Chronicle books and gifts are available at special quantity discounts
to corporations, professional associations, literacy programs, and other organizations.
For details and discount information, please contact our premiums department
at corporatesales@chroniclebooks.com or at 1-800-759-0190.

Chronicle Books LLC
680 Second Street
San Francisco, California 94107

Chronicle Books—we see things differently.
Become part of our community at www.chroniclekids.com.

The Dreamer

Il Sung Na

chronicle books · san francisco

Once, there was a pig who admired birds.

But he could never join them. Could he?

When they flew south, he wanted to follow.

There was much to learn.

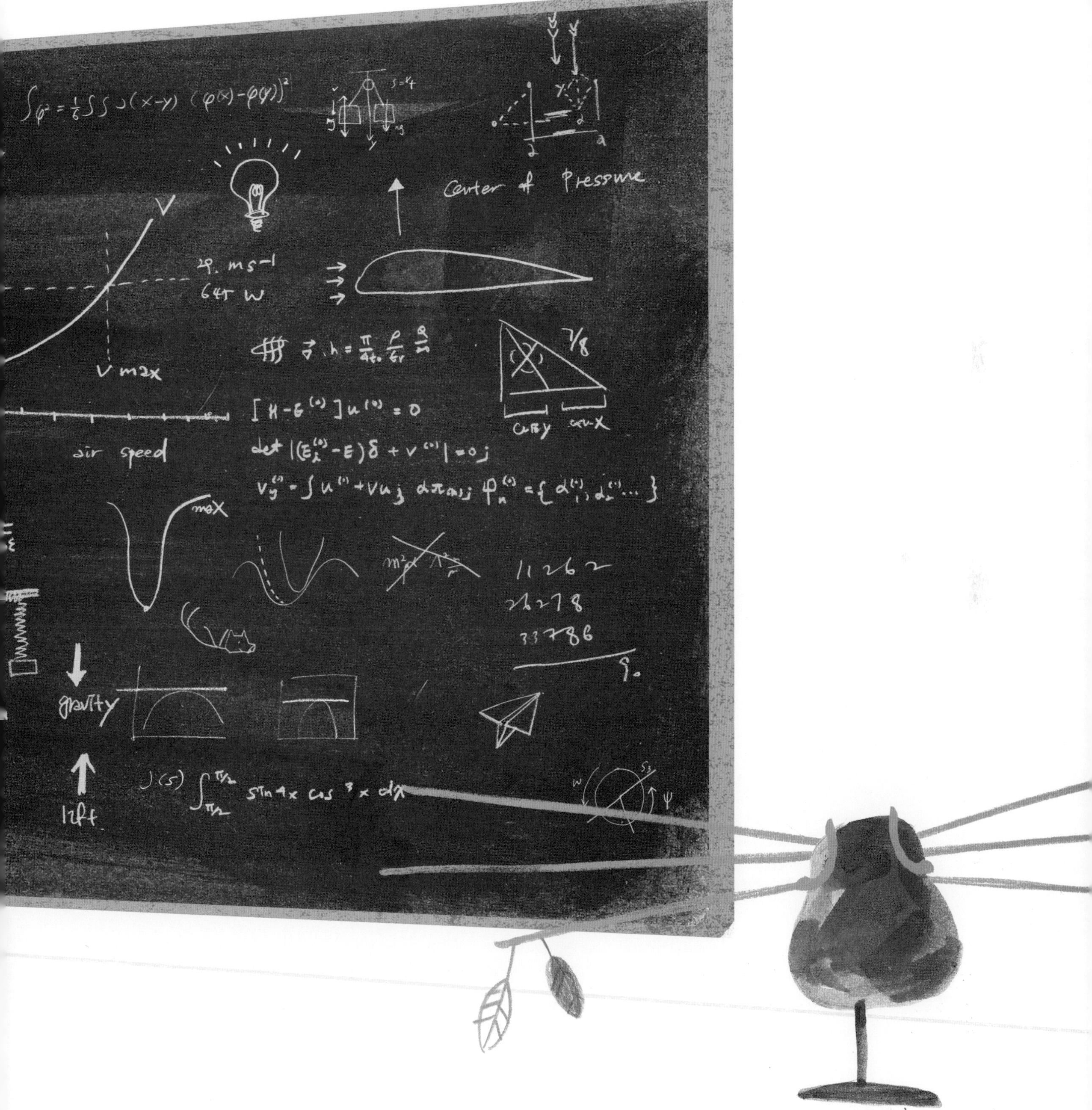
Center of Pressure
v max
air speed
max
gravity
lift

And gather.

But his first flying machines

fell

flat.

He tried . . .

and tried.

He pondered.

And inspiration struck.

His hope blossomed.

But even with help, it was not easy.

So he listened.

Momentum built.

Until one day . . .

He took a running start.

There was no height he couldn't reach.

Was there?

He decided to find out.

Soon the world wanted to join him.

So they did.

Some days everything felt changed.

And some things never would.

Once, there was a pig who admired birds.

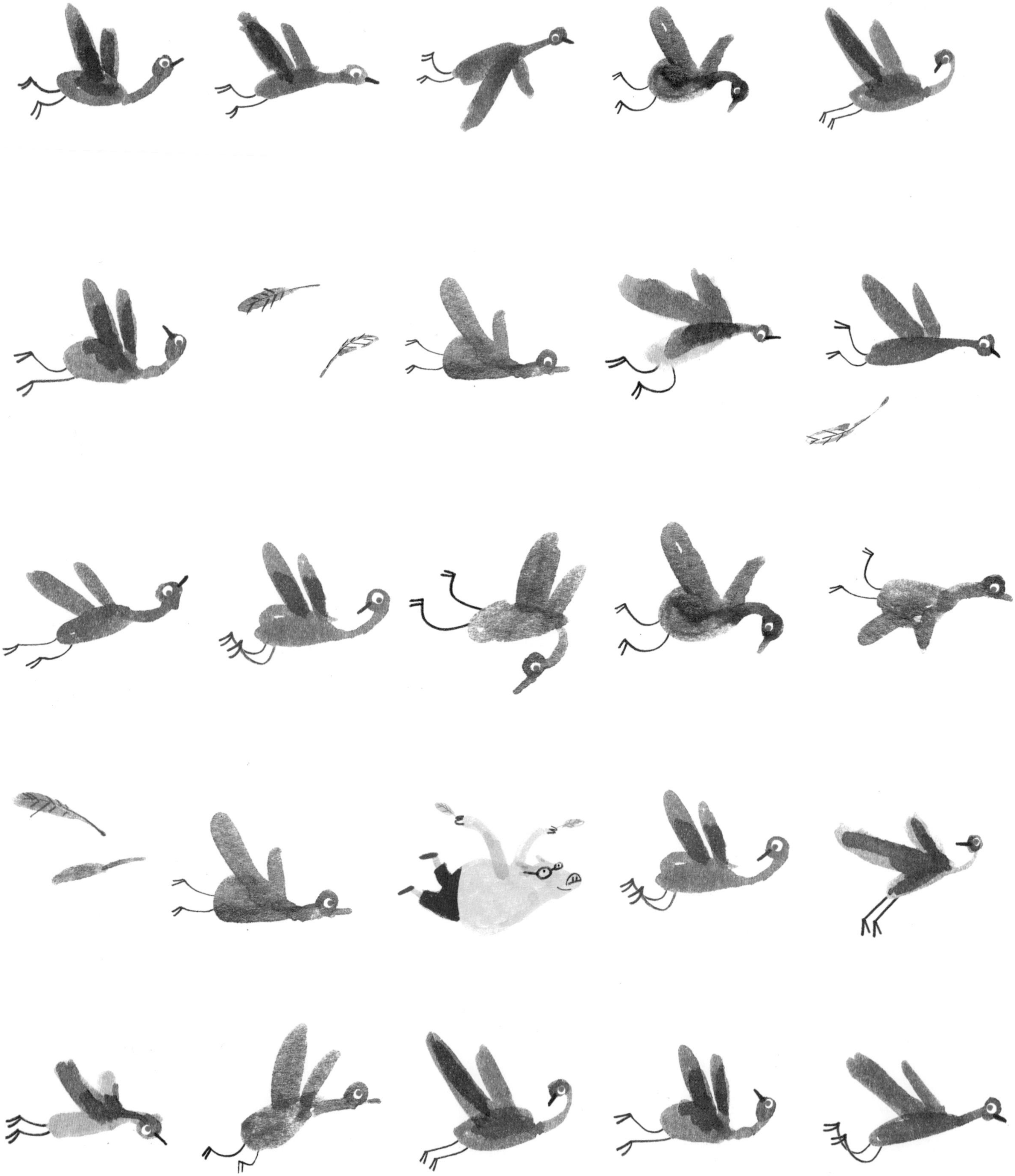